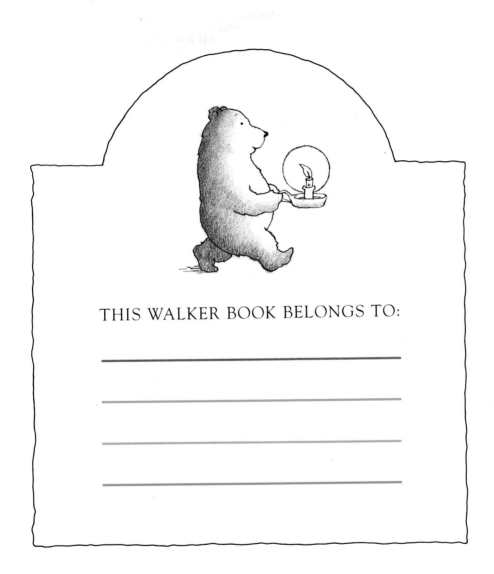

THIS WALKER BOOK BELONGS TO:

ANIMALS AT RISK

For P.R.
J.A.

For Theo
T.H.

The author and publisher wish to thank
Martin Jenkins for his invaluable
assistance in the preparation of this book.

First published 1992 by Walker Books Ltd
87 Vauxhall Walk, London SE11 5HJ

This edition published 1999

2 4 6 8 10 9 7 5 3 1

Text © 1992 Judy Allen
Illustrations © 1992 Tudor Humphries

This book has been typeset in Times New Roman.

Printed in Hong Kong

British Library Cataloguing in Publication Data
A catalogue record for this book is available from the British Library.

ISBN 0-7445-6353-4

PANDA

Written by
Judy Allen

Illustrated by
Tudor Humphries

WALKER BOOKS
AND SUBSIDIARIES
LONDON • BOSTON • SYDNEY

There were four people walking through the damp, misty forest in Western China, but only one of them was Chinese. Lao Meng, a scientist who worked at the research station on the valley floor, was from Beijing.

The other three – two botanists and a twelve-year-old – were from Brooklyn. The twelve-year-old, Jake, was doing his best to pretend he wasn't there at all. When the international group of botanists had planned their expedition, his name had definitely not been on the list.

Then, just before they were due to leave, the filmy-fern expert fell down his porch steps and broke his leg.

No one could be found to take his place so Jake's father – who was part of the team – suggested Jake.

Everybody was so surprised they agreed, and it was not until the plane was in the air that one or two people began to have doubts.

"I hope I'm going to see a panda," said Jake.

"I hope you're not going to run about and tread on rare specimens," said Professor Beall.

"I hope I'm not going to regret this," said Jake's father, who was Professor Beall's assistant.

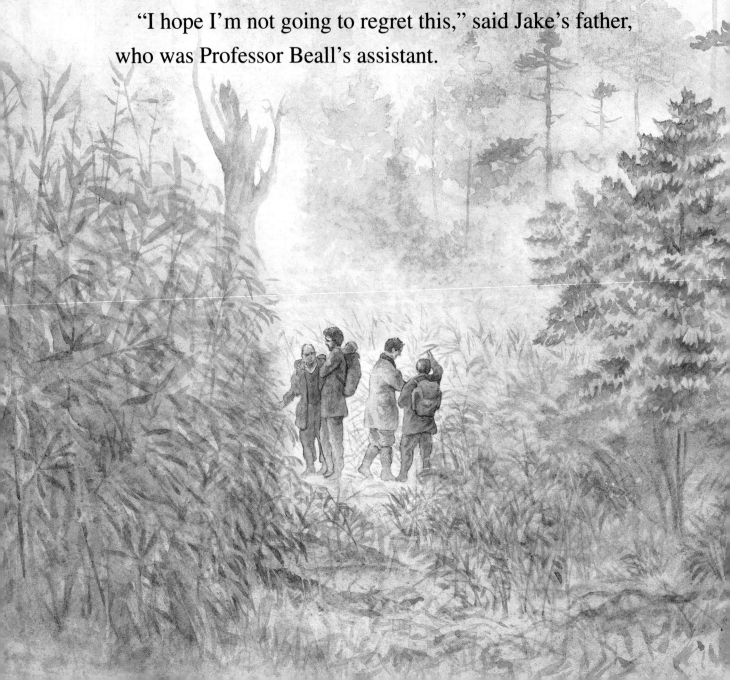

So Jake was being extremely careful not to be a nuisance as they marched through the clammy undergrowth looking at special plants.

Today, Professor Beall had persuaded Lao Meng to lead the three of them away from the main expedition to look for a rare species of orchid. The plan was that Lao Meng would leave them at a remote campsite, in the area where the orchids grew, and return to fetch them a day or so later.

As they walked past mossy-trunked trees, through wet ferns and grasses, and around tough thickets of bamboo, Professor Beall asked Lao Meng complicated questions about plants with Latin names. Lao Meng gave him complicated answers, but he still found time to point out things he thought Jake would find interesting.

Jake especially liked the dove tree, whose flowers hung from its branches like handkerchiefs.

Then Lao Meng showed him the bamboo, whose flowers were so small and pale they looked like shreds of cloth, caught on the stems by accident.

"You're here at the right time," he said. "This species only flowers once every ten years."

"Pandas eat bamboo, don't they?" said Jake, glancing

around, half expecting to glimpse a familiar black and white shape.

"They do," said Lao Meng, "and the flowering is bad news for them. As soon as the seeds drop, the plant dies, and it's a few years before the new plants are big enough for panda-fodder. Luckily there are two different species of bamboo in this area, and the other one won't flower for some years."

He stopped suddenly. "Look!" he said. "Quickly! Across the valley there." He pushed his binoculars at Jake.

"What?" said Jake, taking them. "Is it a panda?"

"No," said Lao Meng. "I can hardly believe it, but it's a mint-leopard – what you call a clouded leopard."

Through the binoculars Jake saw it, climbing head first down the trunk of a tall tree, moving as comfortably as if it were strolling across a meadow, and then dropping to the ground, out of sight.

"Are they dangerous?" said Jake's father anxiously.

"Only to monkeys and squirrels," said Lao Meng. "They keep well away from humans. In ten years of walking through this forest, I've never seen one before. You must have brought me luck."

Later, he pointed out a bright orange and blue pheasant, which he said was called Temminck's tragopan, and a tiny shrew mole that they almost stepped on.

The campsite turned out to be no more than a clearing with a raised wooden platform. Lao Meng left as soon as he had helped put up their tent, and they ate supper as dusk fell, listening to the chirps and shrieks from the forest.

Professor Beall woke them early next morning, when the view from the tent was still all washed away by dawn mist. He wanted to leave at once to look for the orchids, which was what they had expected. What they had not expected, though, was that he wanted to leave Jake behind.

"We'll only be gone a few hours," he said, "and two of us are less likely to tread on delicate plants than three of us would be."

Jake was delighted. He'd had enough of plant hunting and was quite happy to stay in the tent with his personal stereo and his favourite tapes. Jake's father was doubtful, but Professor Beall soon persuaded him.

"He'll be safer here than he was in Brooklyn," he said, as the two men left. "There's no one around, not even any dangerous beasts."

It wasn't until mid-morning that Jake decided to go for a walk. Yesterday they had had the luck to see the leopard. Perhaps today, he thought, he would have the luck to see the one animal he had been dreaming about ever since he'd joined the expedition. Ten minutes from the camp, though, he realized he had made a big mistake. Pushing through the dripping undergrowth all by himself was not at all like following Lao Meng, and even though he couldn't see any creatures, he had a distinct feeling he was being watched. What was worse, when he looked back, the campsite had completely disappeared and for a terrible moment it seemed he was lost for ever in a Chinese forest. He crashed back in what he thought was the right direction, hoping the noise would frighten off any clouded leopard who might be near by.

But when he pushed past a stand of bamboo and saw the tent in front of him, he had a nasty surprise. Someone was inside. He could see the shadows of movement through the canvas walls – and when he stood still he could hear sounds, too.

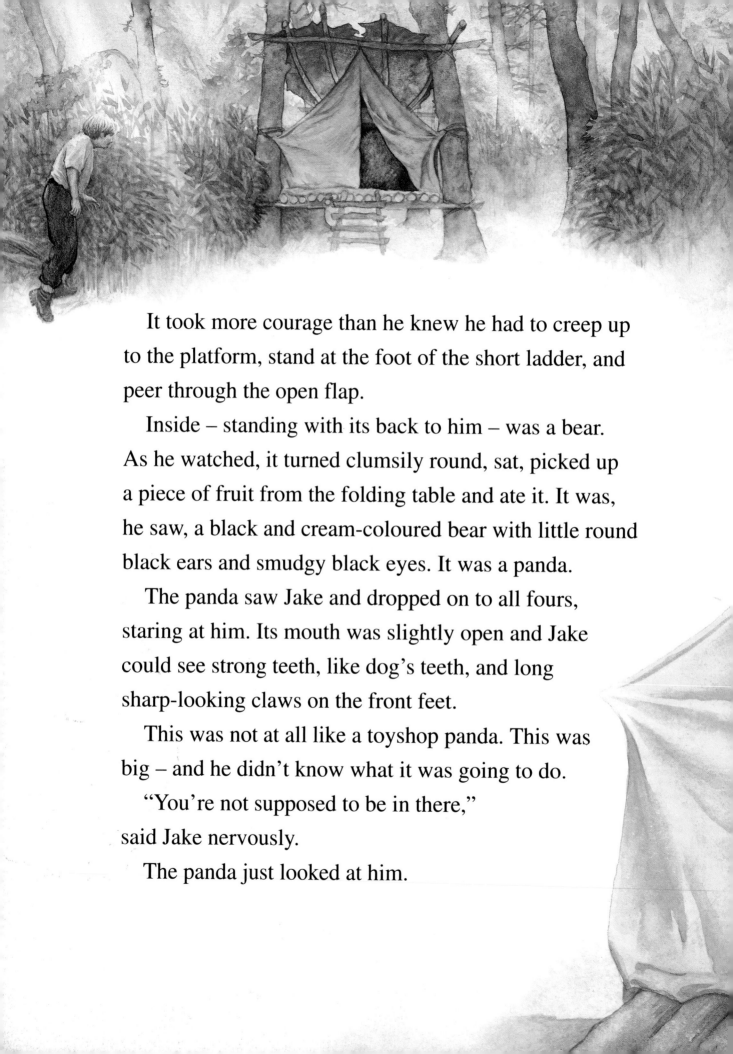

It took more courage than he knew he had to creep up to the platform, stand at the foot of the short ladder, and peer through the open flap.

Inside – standing with its back to him – was a bear. As he watched, it turned clumsily round, sat, picked up a piece of fruit from the folding table and ate it. It was, he saw, a black and cream-coloured bear with little round black ears and smudgy black eyes. It was a panda.

The panda saw Jake and dropped on to all fours, staring at him. Its mouth was slightly open and Jake could see strong teeth, like dog's teeth, and long sharp-looking claws on the front feet.

This was not at all like a toyshop panda. This was big – and he didn't know what it was going to do.

"You're not supposed to be in there," said Jake nervously.

The panda just looked at him.

Jake thought he knew how to lure the panda out of the tent. He went back to the bamboo and picked some stems. They were tough and hurt his hands, but he got a good bunch and carried it back to the steps.

"Come and get it," he said, holding out a stem to the panda.

The panda sat down and continued to look at him. Jake crept closer, still holding out the stem. When he was near enough, the panda took the stem and ate it – grasping it in a hairy paw and turning its head to one side to chew on its back teeth.

Jake's plan to lure the panda out failed completely – instead, the panda lured him in by sitting where it was and reaching out for more bamboo. Jake went to and from the thicket several times. He felt like a waiter going to and from a restaurant kitchen.

After a while, the panda let him scratch it behind the ear with a long stick. Then it let him scratch it with his hand. It even turned slightly towards him and raised its arm so Jake could scratch a particular itch. Later it accepted the rest of the fruit and several hard biscuits and even enjoyed the dried meat.

Jake sat beside it while it ate. It was big and calm and very slightly smelly, its coat much thicker and coarser than he had expected, its eyes quite small in their dark, smudgy surrounds. He couldn't believe it was neither frightened of him nor angry with him.

When it was full, the panda plodded over to Jake's sleeping-bag. It raked it into a comfortable nest with its strong claws, turned round three times, then slumped down and sank into a deep sleep.

Thinking about it later, Jake decided he must have watched it for a good hour before he noticed that Professor Beall had left his spare camera behind. He could see it was an expensive one, but he felt sure the Professor would want him to use it. After all, the panda might have gone by the time the two men returned.

The click from the shutter disturbed the sleeping animal, and it raised its head. When it heard the whirring of the wind-on mechanism it got up and ambled through the tent. Jake put the camera on the table and stood aside.

Just as it reached the tent opening, the panda sat down heavily, half on the table, and scratched. The table collapsed and the camera fell.

The panda flopped down the three steps from the tent platform and plodded off into the forest, rocking a little as it walked.

"Thanks for calling," said Jake, and he meant it. Then he picked up the camera. It was jammed.

"Ah, rats!" said Jake, and he meant that, too.

By the time his father and Professor Beall got back, grinning at the success of their orchid-hunt, he had tidied his torn bedding and set the table on its legs again. But there was no way he could fix the broken camera, or replace the missing food.

They listened to Jake's extraordinary story. Then the Professor shrugged and said, "Cameras can be mended – and most people eat too much when they're bored."

"You don't believe me!" said Jake, horrified. "But it *is* true."

"I was afraid I'd regret bringing you," said his father.

"Forget it," said the Professor. "I blame myself for leaving him alone." He sat down and began to sort through the specimens they'd collected. He was not grinning any more.

Jake's father took Jake aside. "I'm disappointed in you," he said. "You shouldn't have touched the camera – and you should have been more considerate about the food – but I can forgive all that. What I can't forgive is that you should lie about it."

"I'm not lying," said Jake desperately. "Come and look at my bedding – it's got claw marks and panda-hair on it."

His father shook his head. "You're obsessed with pandas," he said. "I have no more to say to you until you tell the truth."

In silence the three of them made a meal with what was left – a vegetable stew with rice. Jake took his a few yards away from the tent and sat on a fallen log. He stared into his bowl, not at all hungry.

"Maybe a camera shop can get the film out and develop it," he said at last. "Then I'll have the picture as proof."

The two men ignored him.

"Lao Meng will believe me," he said, "when he comes to fetch us tomorrow."

They didn't answer.

It was not very long before Jake heard the sounds of someone approaching through the forest. He listened, hopefully. Maybe that's Lao Meng, he thought, come back early. But what if he doesn't believe me, either?

The figure which appeared at the edge of the trees was not Lao Meng, though. It was shorter and stouter and very much hairier.

Three pairs of eyes stared as the panda approached to within a couple of metres of where Jake sat.

The panda looked at Jake.

Jake looked at the panda.

Then, very slowly and gently, Jake held out his bowl. The panda shuffled closer, sniffed, then sat back on its haunches, took it in its paws, and drank the stew.

Then it licked the bowl thoroughly, inside and out. Nobody said a word. Nobody moved.

When the panda had finished, it dropped the bowl, rolled forward on to all fours and shambled slowly off into the trees.

There was a silence which lasted for several seconds.

Then Professor Beall said, very quietly, "We have had an honoured guest."

He got to his feet and walked over to where Jake sat.

"Two honoured guests," he said, holding out his hand to him. "Please forgive me, Jake."

"Jake," said his father, following behind the Professor, "Jake, I'm sorry – I apologize."

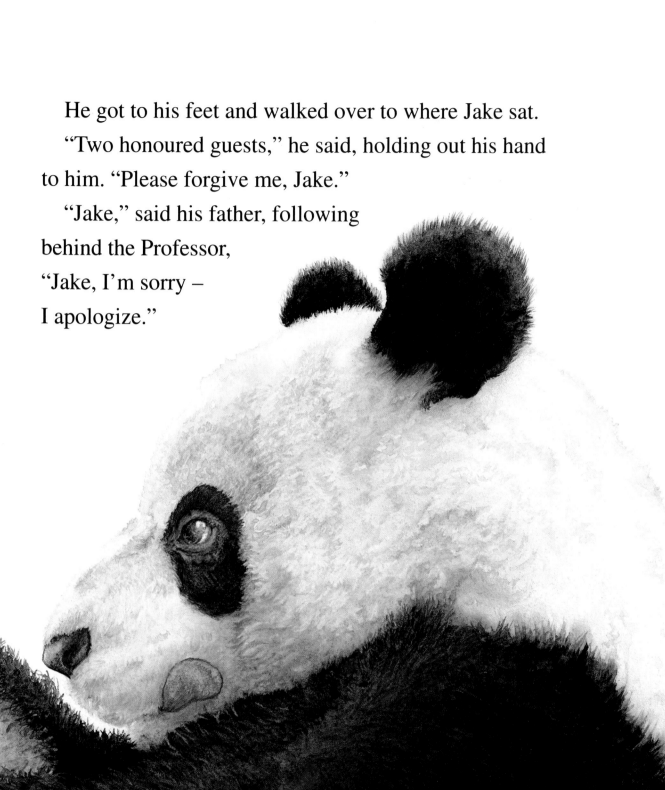

"That's OK," said Jake. "But I still hope my picture comes out. You both forgot to take one."

PANDA FACT SHEET

THE GIANT PANDA is perhaps the best known and most loved of all rare animals. About 1,000 of them survive in the rainy hills of south-west China, in the provinces of Sichuan, Shaanxi and Gansu. Here the pandas feed on various sorts of bamboo which grow in dense thickets on the hillsides.

♦ WHAT ARE THE DANGERS FOR PANDAS? ♦

Every ten or fifteen years the bamboos which the pandas eat all flower at once and then die off after they have produced their seeds. This leaves the pandas with very little to eat until new bamboo plants have grown. In the past, the pandas would move to other areas to find bamboo that was not flowering. In recent years, though, people have cut down so much bamboo to make space for their homes and their crops, that many pandas die of starvation. In addition, pandas are sometimes trapped for their skins, which can be sold for very high prices, or are accidentally caught in snares which poachers have set for other animals.

◆ IS ANYONE HELPING PANDAS? ◆

Yes. The Chinese government has made it illegal to kill them, and has turned most of the areas where they still live into national parks and reserves. Since 1980, WWF (World Wide Fund for Nature) has worked with the Chinese government to find out more about the pandas' habits so that they can be better protected.

◆ ARE EFFORTS TO SAVE PANDAS SUCCEEDING? ◆

Up to a point. Their population is not decreasing, in fact it has remained the same for fifteen years now. However, scientists worry that this population may not be big enough to ensure that the species survives. Pandas prefer to live solitary lives, their courtship rituals are long and complicated, and the females usually only have one cub at a time. This means that the pandas which die from starvation, trapping, or simply old age are not replaced very rapidly. There is a lot more work to do before anyone can say for certain that the panda is safe.

◆ IS THERE ANYTHING YOU CAN DO? ◆

Yes. You can join the junior section of the WWF, or persuade your family or your school to join.

WWF
Panda House
Weyside Park
Godalming
GU7 1XR

◆ ABOUT THE AUTHOR ◆

Judy Allen worked as a book editor before becoming a writer in 1973. Since then she has written many books for children and adults, including the award-winning children's novel, *Awaiting Developments*, as well as compiling Walker Books' *Anthology for the Earth*. Judy Allen lives in London.

About *Panda*, Judy says, "Pandas can be unpredictable and dangerous but there's something comforting about them. That's why the story ends the way it does — with the panda's return bringing about the resolution of the story."

◆ ABOUT THE ILLUSTRATOR ◆

Tudor Humphries lives in Devon with his wife and three children. He has worked as a landscape painter, a children's book illustrator, and a life-drawing teacher. He is also a qualified costume and set designer, and this theatrical training has had a profound effect on his ideas about drama, lighting and atmosphere in pictures.

About *Panda*, Tudor says, "In this book we wanted to get away from the cuddly toy image of the panda and make children aware of it as a naturally wild animal."